teach a **GIRL** to lead

This book is donated by the

Center for American Women and Politics,

The Hess Foundation, and

_____

tag.rutgers.edu

W9-BXV-600

Text copyright © 2008 by Kelly DiPucchio
Illustrations copyright © 2008, 2012 by LeUyen Pham

All rights reserved. Published by Disney • Hyperion, an imprint of Disney Book Group. No
part of this book may be reproduced or transmitted in any form or by any means, electronic
or mechanical, including photocopying, recording, or by any information storage and
retrieval system, without written permission from the publisher. For information address
Disney • Hyperion, 125 West End Avenue, New York, New York 10023-6387.

Revised Edition, March 2012
5 7 9 10 8 6 4
H106-9333-5-15028
This book is set in Caslon Antique.
Printed in Malaysia
ISBN 978-1-4231-3999-7
Reinforced binding
Visit www.DisneyBooks.com

FOR
GRACE,
who asked
the question
"Where are the
girls?"
K.D.

VOTE
GRACE

For
Angelic Ruiz,
★ ★ ★
who I expect to be
president in
thirty-two years
L.P.

FOR
GRACE

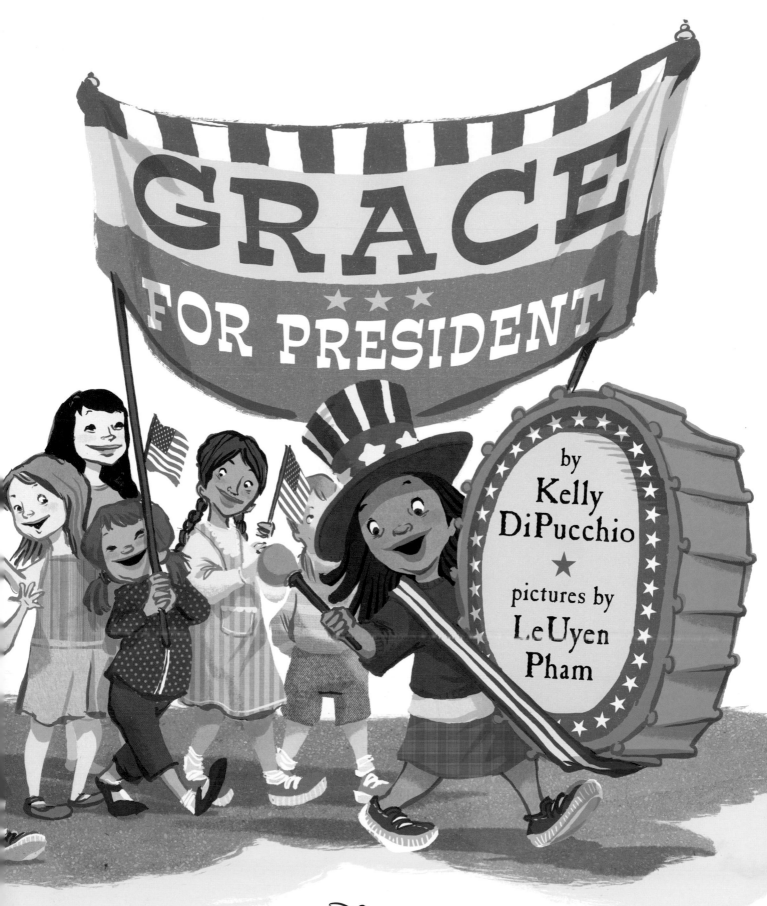

GRACE
★★★
FOR PRESIDENT

by
Kelly
DiPucchio
★
pictures by
LeUyen
Pham

DISNEP · HYPERION
LOS ANGELES NEW YORK

One Monday morning in September, Mrs. Barrington rolled out a big poster with all of the presidents' pictures on it. Grace Campbell could not believe her eyes.

Where are the GIRLS?

"That is a very good question!" said Mrs. Barrington.
"The truth is, our country has never had a woman president."

"NO girl president?
EVER?"
Grace asked.

"No, I'm afraid not,"
said Mrs. Barrington.

Grace sat at her desk
and stewed. No girls?
Who'd ever heard of
such a crazy thing?

Finally, she raised her hand.

"Yes, Grace?"

"I've been thinking it over, and I'd like to be

PRESIDENT!"

Several students in the class laughed.

"Well, I think that's a star-spangled idea, Grace!"
said Mrs. Barrington. "In fact, we can have our own
election right here at Woodrow Wilson Elementary!"

The snickering in the room stopped. Grace smiled.
"Would anyone else like to run for president?"
Mrs. Barrington asked the class.

Nobody raised their hand.

Becoming president was going to be easy! Grace thought.

The next day, Mrs. Barrington made an announcement.

"In the name of DEMOCRACY,
I have invited Mr. Waller's class to join our election.

Their class has nominated
THOMAS COBB
to be their presidential candidate!"

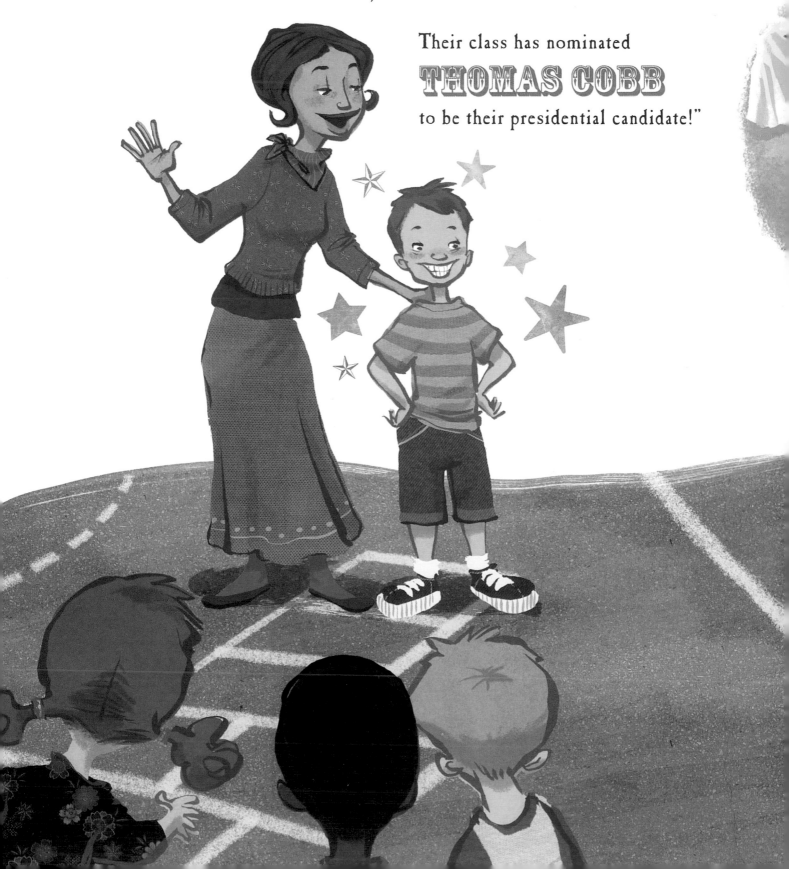

Grace's heart sank.

Thomas was the school
spelling bee champion.
His experiments always took
a blue ribbon at the science fair.
And he was captain of the soccer team.

Becoming president wasn't going to be
so easy, after all, Grace thought.

The teachers put the names of all fifty states and the District of Columbia into a hat. Everyone except for Grace and Thomas got to choose a state.

"I'm Texas!" said Anthony.

"I'm New Hampshire!" said Rose.

"I'm Michigan," said Robbie. "What does the number 16 mean?"

"Each state is assigned a number of electoral votes. That number is determined by how many people live in that state," said Mrs. Barrington. "Each of you will be a representative for your state."

"Altogether, our country has 538 electoral votes," Mr. Waller explained. "On election day, the candidate who receives 270 electoral votes or more wins the election!"

"Why 270?" asked Rose.

"That's more than half of all the electoral votes," Mr. Waller said.

Becoming president REALLY wasn't going to be so easy, Grace thought.

Grace came up with a campaign slogan:

Thomas came up with his own campaign slogan:

Grace listened to what issues were important to the students, and she made a list of campaign promises:

Thomas made up his own list of promises:

Grace made campaign posters and buttons.
Thomas made posters and buttons, too.

Each week, the teachers set aside time for
the candidates to meet with their constituents.

Polls were taken. Voters were making their choices.

Grace continued to campaign.

At recess, she gave SPEECHES.

During lunch, she handed out free CUPCAKES.

After school, she held RALLIES.

MEANWHILE,

Thomas wasn't worried.

THOMAS IS #1

VOTE FOR THOMAS

THOMAS FOR PRESIDENT

Arizona 11
Arkansas 6
California 55
Colorado 9
Connecticut 7
Delaware 3
D.C. 3
Florida 29
Georgia 16
Hawaii 4
Idaho 4
Illinois 20
Indiana 11
Iowa 6
Kansas 6

...tucky 8
Louisiana 8
Maine 4
Maryland 10
Massachusetts 11
Michigan 16
Minnesota 10
Mississippi 6
Missouri 10
Montana 3
Nebraska 5
Nevada 6
New Hampshire 4
New Jersey 14
New Mexico 5
New York 29
N. Carolina 15

N. Dakota 3
Ohio 18
Oklahoma 7
Oregon 7
Pennsylvania 20
Rhode Island 4
S. Carolina 9
S. Dakota 3
Tennessee 11
Texas 38
Utah 6
Vermont 3
Virginia 13
Washington 12
W. Virginia 5
Wisconsin 10
Wyoming 3

271

He had cleverly calculated that the **BOYS** held slightly more electoral votes than the **GIRLS.**

At recess, Thomas studied his spelling words.

During lunch, he worked on his latest science experiment.

After school, he played soccer.

Even before the election, Grace made good on her promises. She joined the safety squad. She organized a school beautification committee, and she volunteered her time in the school cafeteria.

In early November, Woodrow Wilson Elementary hosted a special Election Day assembly. Grace and Thomas took their places onstage as the school band began to play.

Henry was the first representative to approach the microphone.

The Yellowhammer State of Alabama casts its 9 electoral votes for Thomas Cobb!

Fletcher said,

The Last Frontier State of Alaska casts its 3 electoral votes for the best man for the job, Thomas Cobb!

Hannah called out:

The Grand Canyon State of Arizona casts its 11 electoral votes for Grace Campbell!

And so it went. State after state after state cast their electoral votes. The scoreboard in the gymnasium kept track of the totals.

The voting demonstration was quickly coming to an end.
Clara approached the podium.

The Badger State
of Wisconsin casts
its 10 votes for
my best friend,
Grace Campbell!

Grace looked at the scoreboard.
Thomas had 268 electoral votes. She had 267.
There was only one state still unaccounted for.

WYOMING

Thomas grinned. Grace felt sick.
Sam walked up to the microphone.

He looked at Thomas.

He looked at Grace.
He looked down at Grace's handmade flag.

Sam didn't say a word.

"What are you waiting for?"
Thomas whispered.

The band stopped playing.

All eyes were on Wyoming.

Finally, Sam cleared his throat.

The Equality State of Wyoming casts its three electoral votes for...

SPEC___ ___ECTION

268
THOMAS

267
GRACE

The gymnasium eruted in loud cheers
(and a few boos).
Mrs. Barrington approached the podium.
"With 270 electoral votes, the winner is Grace Campbell!"

Thomas looked stunned. Grace hugged Sam.
"Why did you do it?" she asked.
Sam handed Grace his flag. "Because," he said,
"I thought you were the best person for the job."

The following week, students in Mrs. Barrington's class were preparing for their Career Day presentations.

Grace volunteered to go first. She stood at the front of the room and glanced at the poster still hanging on the wall.

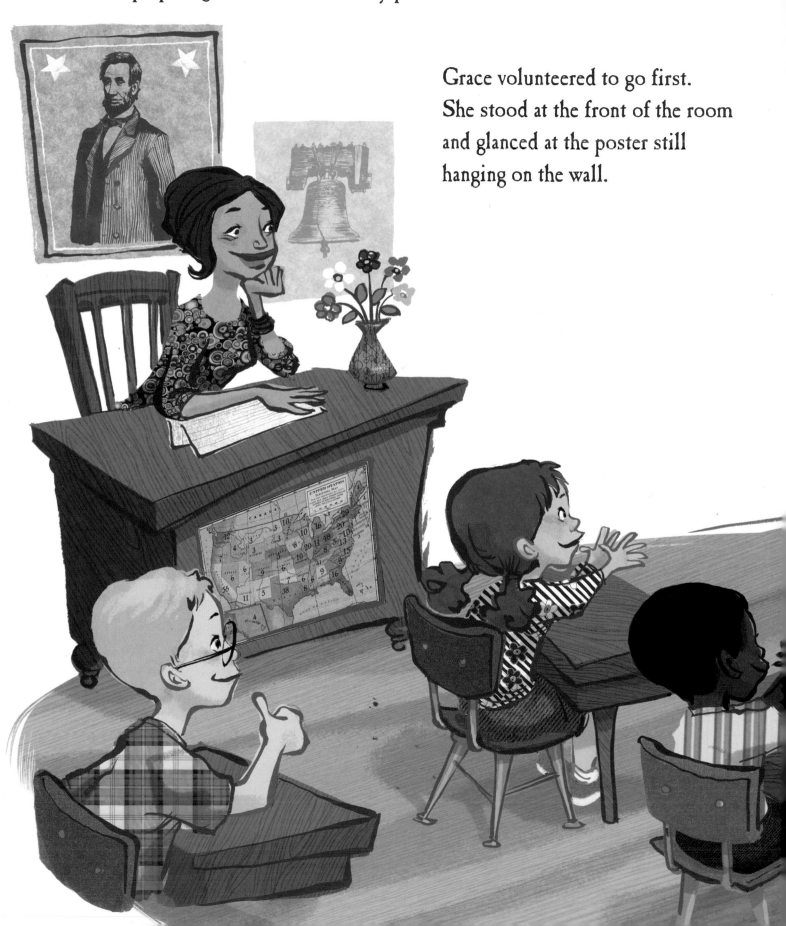

My name is Grace Campbell, and when I grow up, I'm going to be president of the United States.

This time, everyone believed that she would.

★ AUTHOR'S NOTE ★

You might be wondering what the Electoral College is and how it works. You're not alone! Many adults have a hard time understanding the process. First of all, the Electoral College has nothing to do with going to college. It's our country's system for electing a president.

When people vote in presidential elections, what they're really doing is telling the representatives from their states who they'd like to become president of the United States. These elected representatives, known as the "electors," then cast their *electoral* votes for the candidate who received the most *popular* votes in his or her state. Currently there are 538 electors in the United States.

Each state is assigned a number of electoral votes equal to the number of senators and representatives it has. Every state has two senators, but the number of representatives each state has depends on its population. So, the more people a state has, the more electoral votes it has. California, for example, has a large population. It has two senators (just like the other states) and 53 members of the House of Representatives (unlike the other states). Simply put:

2 senators + 53 representatives = 55 electoral votes in the state of California

Likewise, states that are less populated will have fewer representatives and fewer electoral votes. (But since electoral allotments are based on population, they are subject to change every ten years when the US tallies its population—a process referred to as taking census.) In an election, the presidential candidate to win the majority of electoral votes—270—is the winner.

Why does our country use such a complicated system? The Electoral College was written into our Constitution all the way back in 1787. Americans didn't have televisions, radios, or computers back then. It was very difficult for average citizens to be accurately informed about all the candidates who were running for president. The Electoral College system gave elected officials a much bigger role in choosing the president of the United States. Even though most Americans do have access to more information today, a Constitutional amendment would have to be passed in order to change the current system. Hundreds of suggestions for changing the election process have been offered over the years, but so far, not one of them has been approved by Congress.

You might be wondering why regular people should even bother to vote in elections if it's the electoral votes from state representatives that determine which man or woman gets to be president. I'll tell you why! It's those individual votes from regular people that add up to become the *popular* vote in each state. Electors cast all of their electoral votes for the candidates their constituents have given the majority of votes to. So every single vote really is very important!

—*K.D.*